DISCARDED

Bruce County Public Library
1243 Mackenzie Rd.
Port Elgin ON N0H 2C6

LH

MY FIRST GUIDE TO DUCT TAPE PROJECTS

by Marne Ventura and Sheri Bell-Rehwoldt

CAPSTONE PRESS
a capstone imprint

First Facts are published by Capstone Press,
1710 Roe Crest Drive, North Mankato, Minnesota 56003
www.mycapstone.com

Copyright © 2017 by Capstone Press, a Capstone imprint. All rights reserved. No part of this publication may be reproduced in whole or in part, or stored in a retrieval system, or transmitted in any form or by any means, electronic, mechanical, photocopying, recording, or otherwise, without written permission of the publisher.

Library of Congress Cataloging-in-Publication data
Names: Bell-Rehwoldt, Sheri, author. | Ventura, Marne, author.
Title: My first guide to duct tape projects / by Sheri Bell-Rehwoldt and Marne Ventura.
Other titles: First facts. My first guides.
Description: North Mankato, Minnesota : Capstone Press, [2017] | Series: First facts. My first guides | Audience: Ages 6–9. | Audience: K to grade 3. | Includes bibliographical references.
Identifiers: LCCN 2016017483|
ISBN 9781515735939 (library binding)
ISBN 9781515736004 (ebook pdf)
Subjects: LCSH: Tape craft—Juvenile literature. | Duct tape—Juvenile literature. | Handicraft—Juvenile literature. Classification: LCC TT869.7 .B45 2017 | DDC 745.59—dc23
LC record available at https://lccn.loc.gov/2016017483

Editorial Credits
Nikki Potts, editor; Kazuko Collins, designer; Jo Miller, media researcher;
Katy LaVigne, production specialist

Image Credits
All Photos by Capstone Studio: Karon Dubke

Design Elements
Shutterstock: chotwit piyapramote, ExpressVectors, NYgraphic, paullinochka

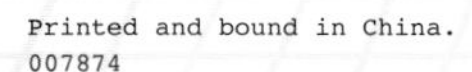
Printed and bound in China.
007874

Table of Contents

Tape It to Make It

Duct tape is strong, flexible, waterproof, and super sticky. People use it to fix everything from boats and chairs to baseball bats. While its useful for fixing things, it's also a great craft supply. So grab a few rolls of duct tape and get ready to make laser swords, treasure chests, bongo drums, and more!

Safety First

Creating duct tape projects should be fun, not painful. Never apply the tape to your body. It could rip out your hair when you peel it off. Apply duct tape over clothing, a towel, a trash bag, or a hat.

You may need to cut through thick layers of duct tape. If using a scissors doesn't work, ask an adult to help you use a utility knife.

Remember to always ask an adult for help when using:

- sharp knives
- scissors
- hot glue guns

Tools and Materials

You'll need some common tools to make many of your projects. Gather the following items so they're easy to find when you need them.

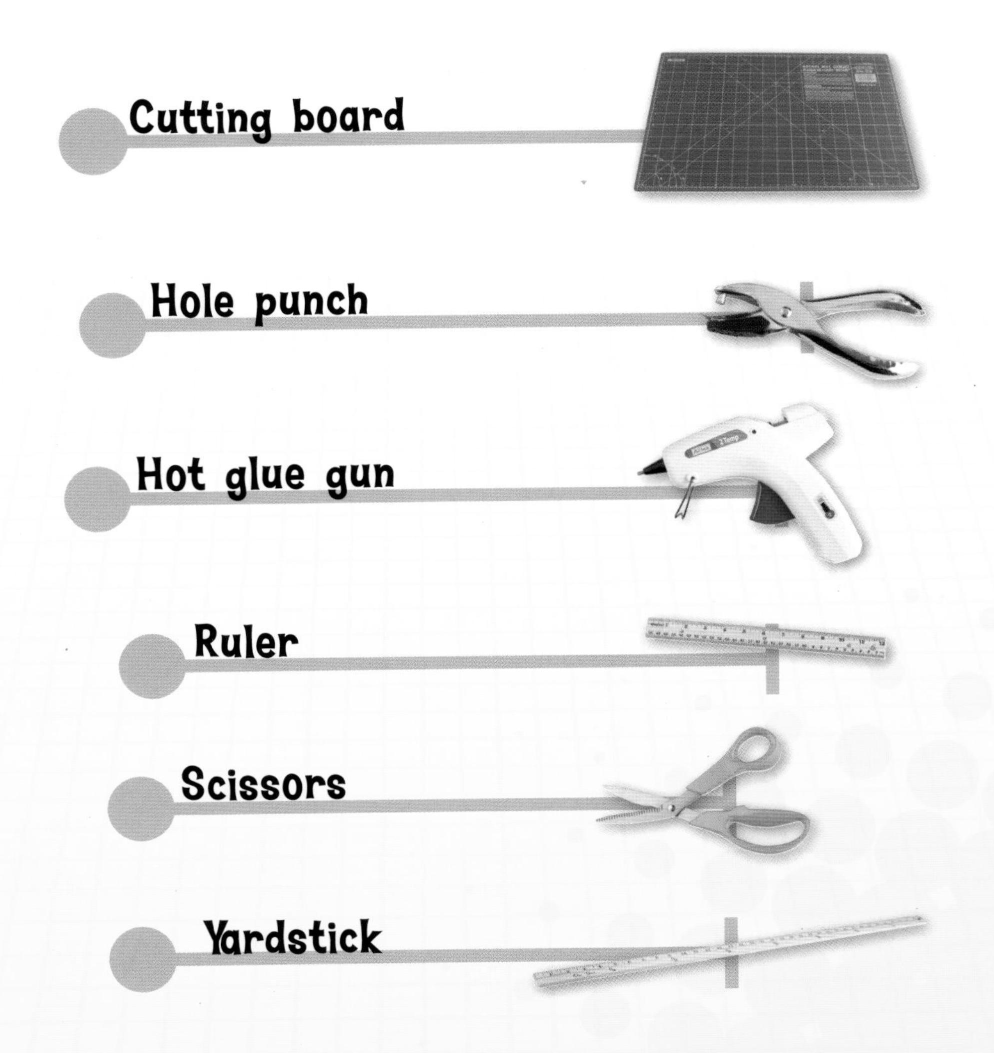

Laser Sword

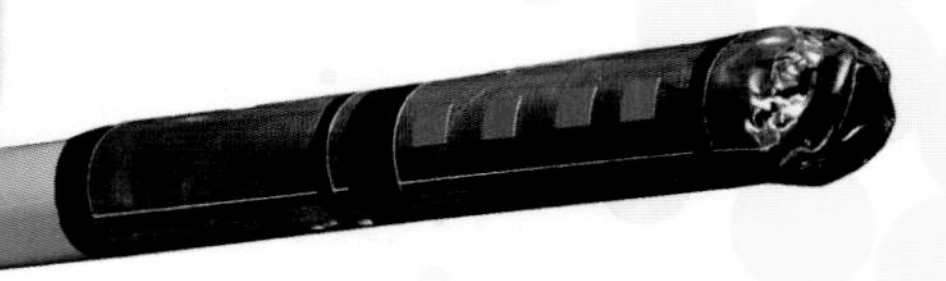

Heading out to battle evil aliens? Smart space warriors never leave home without their trusty laser sword.

MATERIALS

- glow-in-the-dark duct tape
- silver duct tape
- black duct tape
- red duct tape
- scissors
- hot glue gun
- ruler
- cutting board
- 40-inch (102-centimeter) long cardboard giftwrap tube
- 9-inch (23-cm) long cardboard paper towel tube
- two 12- by 12-inch (30- by 30-cm) squares of aluminum foil

Step 1

Crumple one square of aluminum foil into a ball about as wide as the long tube. Use hot glue to secure the foil ball halfway inside the end of the tube.

Step 2

Cover the rounded end of the tube with two 4-inch (10-cm) long strips of glow-in-the-dark duct tape. Then cover the rest of the tube with long strips of glow-in-the-dark tape.

Step 3

Crumple the second square of foil into a ball. Hot glue it to one end of the short tube. Cover the round end with two 4-inch (10-cm) long strips of silver duct tape. Then cover the length of this tube with silver duct tape.

Step 4

Cut two or three 5-inch (13-cm) long strips of black duct tape in various widths. Use these to add stripes to the short tube.

Step 5

Tape four small squares of red duct tape onto the short tube to make buttons, switches, and controls.

Try giving your laser sword 3-D buttons, switches, and controls. Use hot glue to attach craft foam cutouts to the handle. Then cover them with squares of colored duct tape.

Step 6

Slide the short tube onto the open end of the long tube. If it doesn't fit snugly, use hot glue to keep it in place. Now you're ready to save the galaxy!

Book Cover

Book covers don't have to be boring brown. Duct tape book covers offer protection and give your books a unique look.

MATERIALS

- duct tape
- scissors
- book
- ruler
- cutting board
- paper grocery bag

TIP

Use different colored tape to create a pattern on the book cover.

Step 1

Cut down the long side of the bag. Cut off the flat bottom of the bag.

Step 2

Lay the bag flat on the table. Place your book in the middle of the bag. Fold in the top and bottom edges of the paper bag. They should be slightly longer than the top and bottom edges of your book.

Step 3

Fold the left edge of the bag around the front cover of the book. Then slip the front cover into the flap created by the top and bottom folds. Repeat for the back cover of the book.

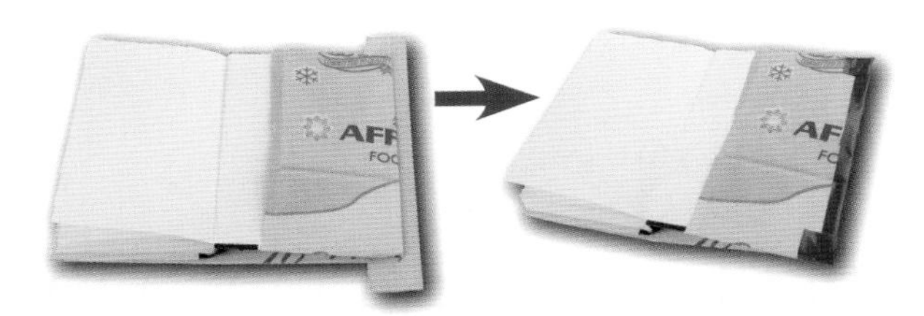

Step 4

Lay a piece of duct tape 2 inches (5 cm) longer than the height of your book along the cover's right edge, sticky side up. Leave 1 inch (2.5 cm) hanging off in all directions. Fold the edges into the inside of the book cover.

Step 5

Slip the book out of the book cover so you don't accidentally tape the book. Continue adding duct tape strips to the outside of the cover. Overlap the strips by 0.25 inches (0.6 cm).

Step 6

Finish covering the back edge with duct tape. Slip the book back inside and your cover is complete!

Bongo Drums

Every band needs a drummer! Use this set of bongo drums to play some great music with your friends.

MATERIALS

- 1 medium oatmeal container
- 1 large oatmeal container
- white duct tape
- tan duct tape
- black duct tape
- scissors
- ruler
- hot glue gun
- cutting board
- brass fasteners
- small block of wood, 2 by 1.5 by 1.5 inches (5 by 3.8 by 3.8 cm)
- hole punch

Step 1

Remove the lids and turn the containers upside down. Cover the bottoms of the containers with white duct tape. Strips should overlap the sides of the containers about 1 inch (2.5 cm). Cover the sides of the drums with vertical stripes of tan and black duct tape.

Step 2

Cut a strip of white tape long enough to fit around the drum with a 2-inch (5-cm) overlap. Fold it in half lengthwise with the sticky sides together. Make two strips for each drum.

Step 3

Punch small holes through the center of the white strips. Measure and mark about 1.5 inches (3.8 cm) from the top and bottom edges of each drum. Attach the white strips around the containers at the marks with a bit of tape. Push brass fasteners through the holes and into the drum. Flatten the fasteners inside the drums.

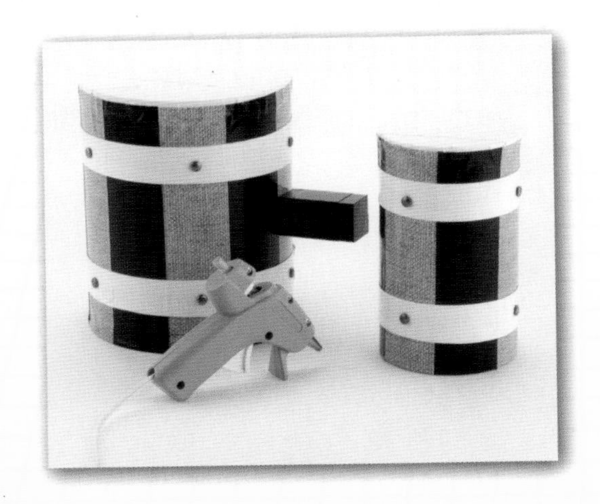

Step 4

Cover the block of wood with a piece of black duct tape. Hot glue the two drums on each side of the wood block. Now you're ready to lay down some awesome beats!

TIP

Coffee cans and cornmeal containers make good drums too. For the best sound, leave the bottom of the drum open.

Treasure Chest

Aarrr! Shiver me timbers! Every pirate needs a safe place to store secret loot. Keep land lovers from snooping into your stuff with this duct tape treasure chest.

MATERIALS

- ruler
- scissors
- cutting board
- plain cardboard box with hinged lid
- wood grain duct tape
- black duct tape
- brass fasteners
- large washer
- small padlock

TIP

If you can't find a box with a hinged lid, you can use a regular shoe box with a lid. Cut away the overhang on one long side of the lid. Then attach it to the box with black duct tape.

Step 1

Cover the box and lid with wood grain duct tape.

Step 2

Use black duct tape to cover the edges of the box. Make a black stripe down the center of the box as well.

Step 3

Measure and make several evenly spaced marks along all of the black stripes. Use the brass fastners to punch small holes into the box at each mark.

Step 4

On the inside of the box, bend the ends of the fasteners out flat.

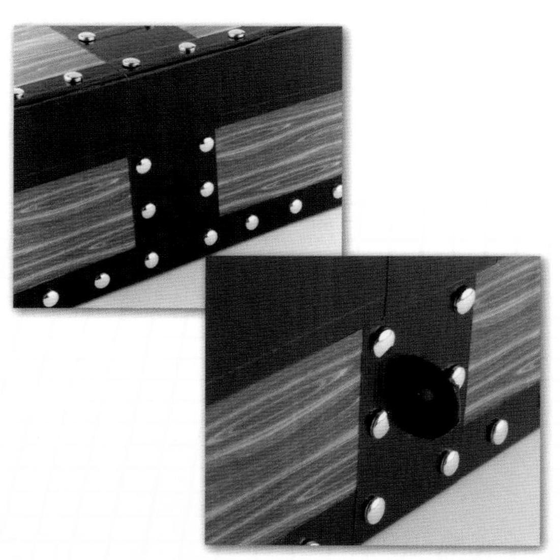

Step 5

Make a 1-inch (2.5-cm) long mark at the front center of the box, just under the lid. Cut a slit at this mark.

Step 6

Cover the washer with black duct tape leaving the hole open in the middle. Use hot glue to attach the washer in place inside the slit in the box.

Step 7

Create a 2- by 3-inch (5- by 7.5-cm) piece of duct tape fabric by overlapping strips of duct tape. Then place strips of tape sticky side down to cover the first layer. Cut a slit in the piece to fit over the washer on the front of the box. Attach this piece inside the front center of the lid. Now just add your secret loot and lock it up to keep it safe!

Flower

Do you want to cheer up a friend when he or she is feeling down? Send them duct tape roses! Unlike the real thing, these blooms will last forever.

MATERIALS

- **plastic drinking straw**
- **green duct tape**
- **another colored duct tape**
- **cutting board**
- **scissors**
- **ruler**

Stem

Step 1

Cut a piece of green duct tape slightly longer than your straw.

Step 2

Lay the tape flat on a table with the sticky side up. Lay the straw along one of the long edges of the tape. Roll the straw toward the opposite edge so that the tape tightly wraps around the straw.

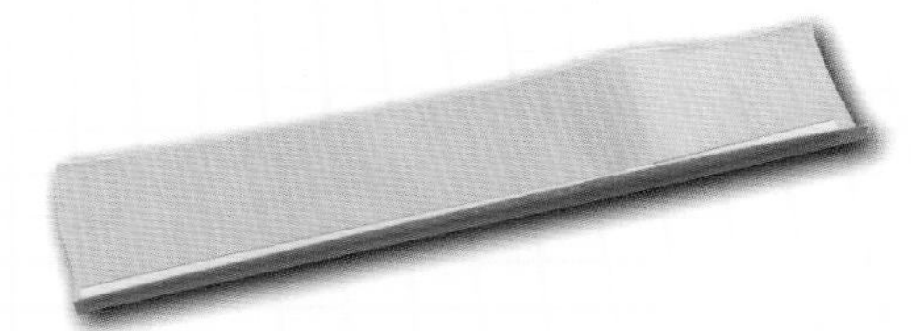

Rosebud

Step 1

Cut a 3-inch (7.6–cm) piece of colored duct tape. Lay it down with the sticky side up. Fold the top corners in until they meet in the middle.

Step 2

Wrap the sticky side of the tape around the end of the straw with the point facing up. This is your rosebud.

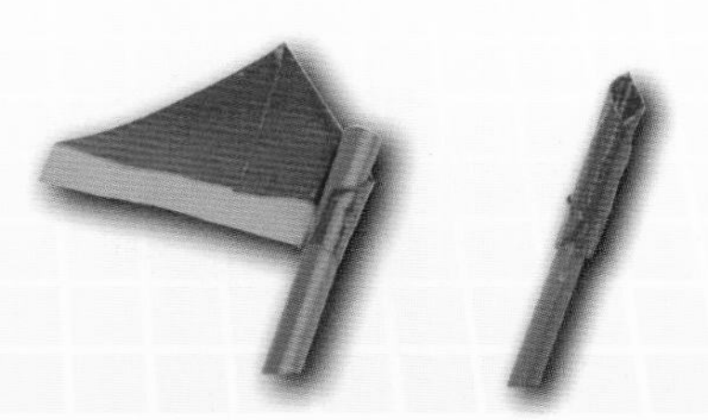

Petals

Step 1

Cut a 3-inch (7.6-cm) piece of colored duct tape the same color as the rosebud. Lay it down with the sticky side up. Fold the top edge down, leaving a small amount of sticky tape showing.

Step 2

Cut the folded edge in an arch shape. Tape the petal around the base of the rosebud.

Step 3

Repeat steps 1 and 2 to make more petals. Stagger the petals as you put them on. Ten petals is usually enough to make a beautiful rose.

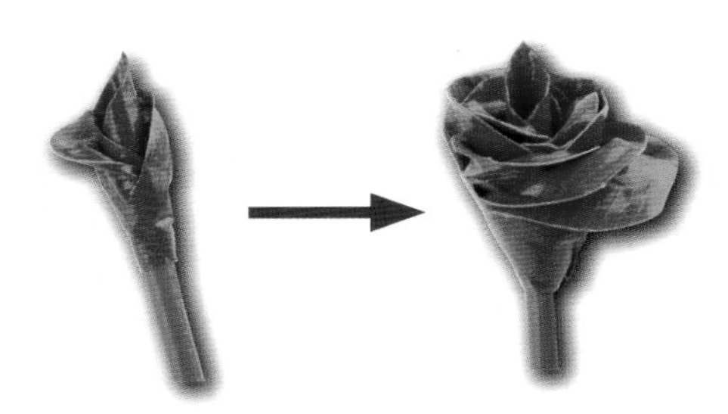

TIP

To give your flowers fragrance, spritz them with perfume.

Leaves

Step 1

Cut a 3-inch (7.6-cm) piece of green duct tape. Lay it down with the sticky side up. Fold the top corners in until they meet in the middle. This will be a leaf.

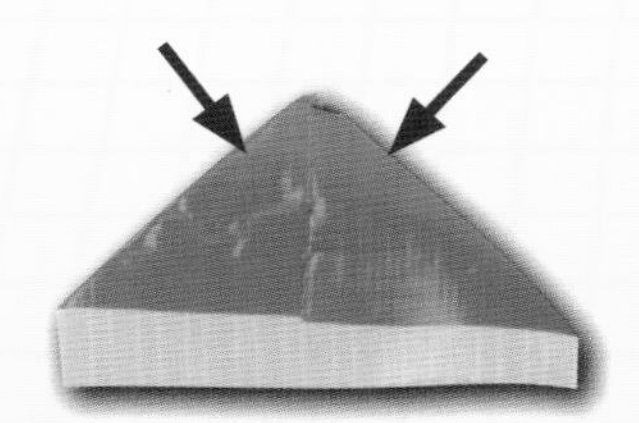

Step 2

You will need two or three leaves to cover the base of the flower petals. Attach the leaves to the base of the flower.

Picture Frame

The best part of taking pictures is displaying them. You can combine old birthday cards with duct tape to create your own picture frames.

MATERIALS

- duct tape
- greeting card
- string
- photo
- pencil
- ruler
- cutting board
- scissors

TIP

You can decorate the frame with glitter, markers, or stickers.

Step 1
Make sure your card is at least 0.5 inches (1.3 cm) longer and wider than your photo. Open the card. Lay the photo in the middle, and trace around it.

Step 2
Remove the photo and draw a second rectangle inside the first. It should be about 0.25 inches (0.6 cm) smaller. Cut along the inner line to make a hole for your photo.

Step 3

Cover the front and back of the card entirely in duct tape. Wrap the tape carefully around the inner edges of the photo hole.

Step 4

Tape your photo inside the hole with the image facing out. Slip the string through the fold of the card, and fold the card shut.

Step 5

Tape the bottom edges and one side of the card together. Leave the other side open so you can easily change your photo whenever you want to. Tie the ends of the string in a knot. Now you're ready to hang your picture!

Checkerboard

Need something fun to do on a long car trip? Turn a clean pizza box into a cool checkers set before you hit the road.

MATERIALS

- clean 10- by 10-inch (25- by 25-cm) pizza box
- scissors
- ruler
- cutting board
- 24 water bottle caps
- black duct tape
- red duct tape
- yardstick

TIP

You can also make checker pieces by covering cardboard circles with red and black duct tape.

Step 1

Cut a 14-inch (36-cm) long strip of red duct tape. Fold it in half lengthwise with the sticky sides together. Repeat this step to make eight red strips and eight black strips.

Step 2

Lay the eight strips of red tape side-by-side on a flat surface. Use a strip of tape to hold them down on one end. Weave the black strips through the red strips to form a checkerboard.

Step 3

Place red tape on the sides of the checkerboard to hold everything in place. Trim each side so it's 1 inch (2.5 cm) wider than the checkerboard.

Step 4

Use red tape to attach the checkerboard to the top of the pizza box. Use black tape to cover the sides of the pizza box.

Step 5

Cut 1- by 1-inch (2.5- by 2.5-cm) squares of duct tape. Make 12 red squares and 12 black squares. Stick the squares to the tops of the bottle caps and smooth the corners down. Cut 0.25- by 4-inch (0.6- by 10-cm) strips of red and black duct tape. Use these to cover the sides of the caps. Trim off any excess tape. Store the checkers inside the box.

Kite

What do Benjamin Franklin and Charlie Brown have in common? They both flew kites! Become a member of the kite flyers club by making your own duct tape kite.

MATERIALS

- 1/8-inch (0.3-cm) wide dowel, 36 inches (91 cm) long
- 1/8-inch (0.3-cm) wide dowel, 33 inches (84 cm) long
- black marker
- large spool of strong string
- colorful duct tape
- large plastic garbage bag
- scissors
- ruler
- cutting board
- yardstick

TIP

Use colorful tape to make your kite stand out in the sky.

Step 1

Measure 10 inches (25 cm) starting from the top of the longer dowel and make a mark. Measure and mark the exact center of the shorter dowel.

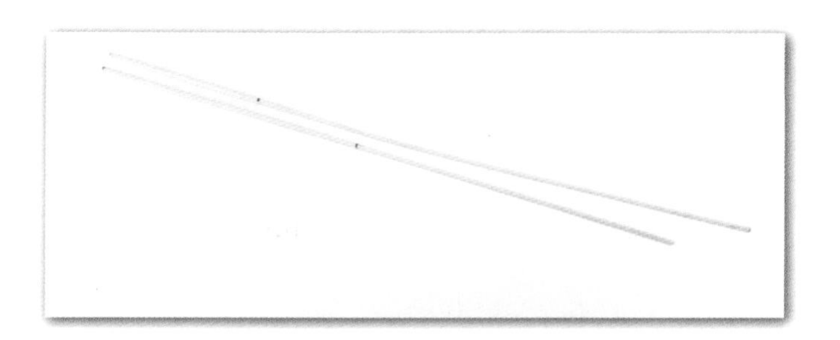

Step 2

Place the dowels together where they are marked to form a "t" shape. Cut a 12-inch (30.5-cm) long piece of the string. Start 3 inches (8 cm) from the end of the string and wind it around the point where the dowels cross. Tightly wind the string around both dowels in a repeating "X" pattern. Tightly tie the two ends of the string together. To make the connection extra sturdy, wrap a small piece of duct tape around the string.

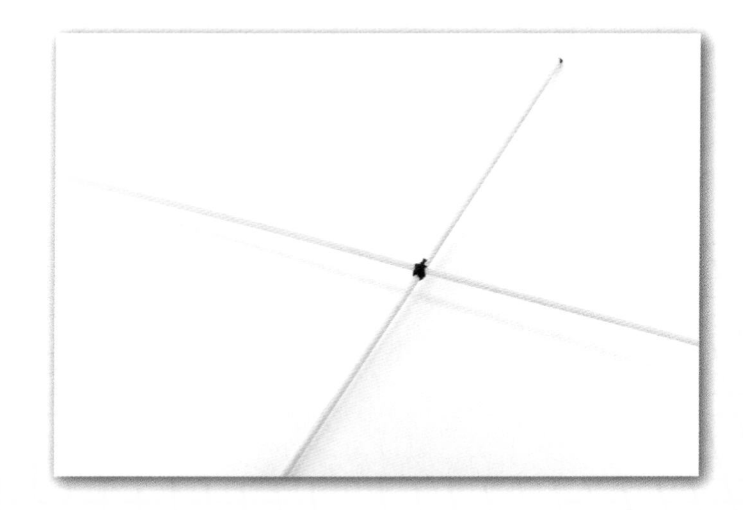

Step 3

Cut two sides of the garbage bag so it is a single sheet of plastic. Lay the kite frame on the sheet of plastic. Draw a kite shape around the frame with the marker. Leave a 1-inch (2.5-cm) wide margin beyond the ends of the dowels.

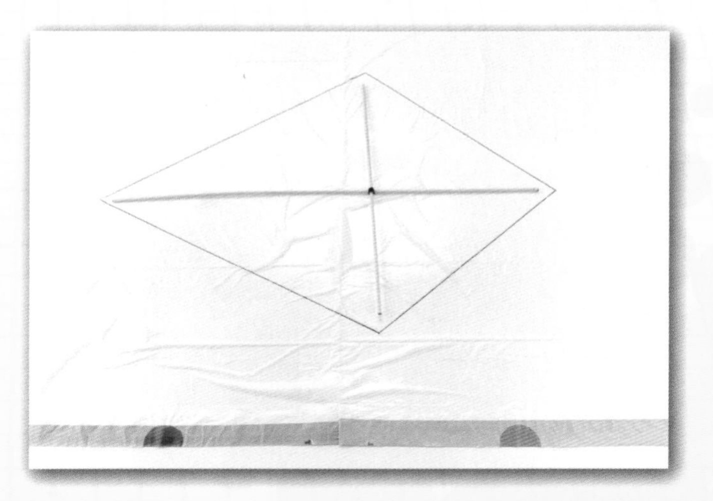

Step 4

Turn over the plastic sheet. Cover the plastic where the kite shape is drawn with strips of duct tape. Be sure to overlap the strips by 0.25 inch (0.6 cm).

Step 5

Flip the plastic over again. Cut out the kite shape. Lay the kite frame on the kite and tape the dowels in place. Fold in the margin around the edges of the kite and over the ends of the dowels. Tape the edges down with small strips of duct tape. Make the corners neat by folding them in before folding in the sides.

Step 6

On the horizontal dowel, make marks 6 inches (15 cm) from the vertical dowel on each side. Punch small holes through the kite at both marks.

Step 7

Tie the end of a 28-inch (71-cm) long piece of string to the horizontal dowel at one mark. Thread the string through the holes in the kite. Tie the other end of the string to the horizontal dowel at the second mark.

Step 8

Cut an 18-inch (46-cm) long piece of duct tape in half lengthwise. Stick the end of one piece onto the second to make a 36-inch (91-cm) long piece. Fold the tape in half lengthwise to make a tail.

Step 9

Cut six 6-inch (15-cm) long pieces of duct tape in half lengthwise. Place them on the tail 5 inches (13 cm) apart with the sticky sides together and the tail sandwiched between them. Then tape the tail to the bottom of the kite.

Step 10

Tie the spool of flying string to the center of the front string on the kite. Now find a wide open, windy space to fly your new kite!

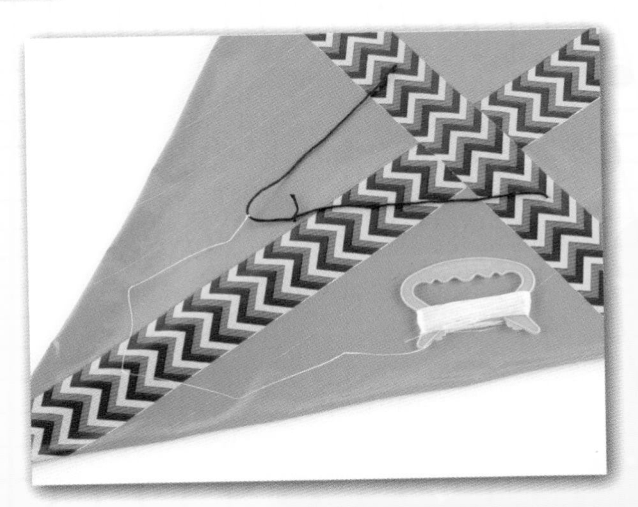

Read More

Formaro, Amanda. *Duct Tape Mania: Crafts, Activities, Facts, and Fun!* White Plains, N.Y.: Studio Fun International, Inc., 2014.

Morgan, Richela Fabian. *Tape It and Make It: 101 Duct Tape Activities.* Tape It And...Duct Tape. Hauppauge, N.Y.: Barron's, 2012.

Ventura, Marne. *Big Book of Building: Duct Tape, Paper, Cardboard, and Recycled Projects to Blast Away Boredom.* Imagine It, Build It. Mankato, Minn.: Capstone Press, 2016.

Internet Sites

FactHound offers a safe, fun way to find Internet sites related to this book. All of the sites on FactHound have been researched by our staff.

Here's all you do:

Visit www.facthound.com

Type in this code: 9781515735939

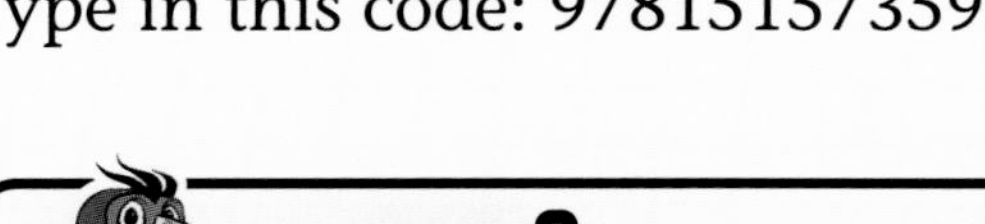

Check out projects, games and lots more at **www.capstonekids.com**

Bruce County Public Library
1243 Mackenzie Rd.
Port Elgin ON N0H 2C6